Big Cat Challenge

Sam Finden

DEDICATION

To Bapa. Thank you for taking us into the woods.
Your grandkids love you very much.

From the Author

As a kid, my imagination ran wild. When my cousin, Skip Johnson, and I were in the woods, we turned into Davy Crockett. My BB gun was instantly transformed into Old Betsy, and we dared any wild critter to mess with us.

Now my imagination sometimes takes a back seat to reality. I live in the mountains, though, where adventures lie behind every downed tree. For a few fleeting moments every so often, Davy Crockett is alive and well in my boots.

As you read *Big Cat Challenge*, I hope you feel the way your ten-year-old self would have. Everyone should be so lucky.

Keep your heels down,

Sam Finden

"Be sober, be vigilant; because your adversary the devil, as a roaring lion, walketh about, seeking whom he may devour."

1 Peter 5:8

Chapter One

A faint noise, barely audible to all but the most highly-trained woodsman's ear, caught Daniel's attention. It made him immediately take in his surroundings, searching out the potential danger. He listened for the echoes and reflections of sound off the nearby boulders.

He froze instinctively, not moving an inch. For five minutes he stood, his muscles quivering with fatigue, deciphering every sound from the last one, then from the next. A cool breeze rustled what was left of last fall's dry aspen leaves, sending them skittering across the exposed granite. They seemed especially loud at the moment; he silently willed the wind to stop.

After determining that his ears may have played a trick on him, he slowly continued on his way. His first few steps were neither smooth nor graceful on muscles suddenly forced into expansion and contraction after having been locked up like a statue. A few yards down the trail, he regained his usual athletic balance and carried on, keeping a watchful eye for anything out of the ordinary.

Daniel Foss had spent the last two weeks creeping around this particular plot of land in northwestern Wyoming, learning all that he could about the landscape. He climbed up to the highest peak—above the tree line—where pockets of snow still peeked out from shady holes between north-facing rocks. He stalked through each thick drainage, where spring-fed streams tumbled over rocks and occasionally disappeared beneath the ground, only to reappear further down the slope.

For fourteen days he observed the way the resident animals interacted with nature. He came to recognize patterns in the mule deer, chipmunks, and blue grouse. He even watched the magpies and Canadian jays. Each species had its own routine, and any diversion from that routine was a symptom of something else.

As a hunter, Daniel knew that more information was always better information. Hunting in new country was a mystery that needed to be solved. Each movement of an animal was a clue. The more clues he had, the sooner he could figure out the riddle.

Daniel's scouting was like detective work. He had to find some leads, follow up on them, then see if they wound up helping him crack the case. At the end of each day, he documented what he'd seen in a journal. He also made corresponding waypoints on a large topographic map. After two weeks, Daniel had a lot of clues.

Since graduating from high school in Mandan, North Dakota, Daniel had made his living—a good living—traipsing around the country, providing a valuable service to developers, farmers, logging outfits, and anyone else with enough money and aggravation to call on him. Daniel was a predator hunter.

It was an unusual line of work, particularly for a young adult. His career started in his teens when a local farmer asked him to take care of a few raccoons. The masked bandits were causing trouble around the farmer's place, getting into his garbage and scattering it around the yard. Daniel's payment then had been exclusive deer hunting, which was a big deal. It ruffled the feathers of some old-timers in town who had, for years, filled their deer tag on that ground. They insisted that Daniel had taken advantage of the farmer.

Daniel saw things differently. The farmer had a problem which, clearly, he couldn't solve on his own. Daniel came up with a solution, and for that he expected to be compensated.

He sold the farmer on it over a slice of warm apple pie in the farmhouse kitchen.

"It won't cost you a thing," Daniel had said.

Even at sixteen, he knew that many farmers were on a tight budget, with most of their money tied up by equipment and land payments. Offering something valuable like varmint eradication for no out-of-pocket expense was a deal too sweet for the farmer to pass up.

The agreement was finalized with a handshake, and both parties hoped for the best.

Two weeks later, the garbage stopped blowing across the farmyard. And two months after that, Daniel pulled into the man's driveway with a big whitetail buck in the bed of his truck.

The arrangement had worked out just as they both hoped.

It was a valuable lesson in running a business for Daniel: if the deal was a good one, both parties wound up feeling satisfied. From then on, Daniel sought out creative opportunities using his hunting skills to help landowners with their problems.

Chapter Two

When he graduated from high school, Daniel loaded his pickup with all his gear and headed down the road, drumming up business in the most grassroots way possible. He went from farm to farm on gravel roads, knocking on doors and meeting people. For a rough-around-the-edges kid from the prairie of North Dakota, this was no small task. Not only was he in unfamiliar country, but he was asking complete strangers to trust him enough to hire him. All through school, he'd been a shy young man. Now, he had no choice but to promote himself.

Whenever he did happen upon a farmer who

was home and needed his services, they balked at the idea of paying him before he'd proven his worth. After being turned down by two different people, Daniel came up with another approach: he would charge them nothing at the start, but would keep all the pelts, along with any shed antlers or winterkill skulls that he found.

The pelts could be sold to fur buyers, who would either sell them to garment makers in the immediate vicinity or send them on to a major fur auction in Canada. Prime furs, if stretched and dried in the same way that the pioneering mountain men had done it for centuries, were worth a bundle. Bobcats and western coyotes were in fashion overseas, particularly in Russia, and they fetched top dollar when demand was high.

Additionally, the antlers could be sold in a number of ways. There were buyers who travelled from county to county and paid by the pound.

These men supplied interior decorators, custom craftsmen, and dog treat companies with all the horns they could ever want. There were drastically different rates for brown, white, or old, chalky horns.

Big sets of shed antlers were also worth a good sum to taxidermists, who would display them with an extra cape on a shoulder mount, then sell it to an interior decorator in one of the resort towns. Often, the owners of big chalet-style homes in trendy mountain towns wanted to show their guests a trophy. To some of them, it made no difference who had killed the animal— they just wanted the mount above their fireplace.

Daniel's favorite stream of income, though, came from scavenging dead heads and selling them. Rarely, he would happen across a dead buck or bull, its bones picked clean by birds or coyotes. He loved to sit and ponder the animal, to think about the circumstances leading up to its demise. Some were obvious, but some were a bit of a mystery.

One time in South Dakota, he found remnants of a longhorn cow skeleton half-buried in the sediment of a dry creek bed at the bottom of a steep canyon wall. Daniel had been looking for rattlesnakes along the base of the cliff when he tripped over a protruding bone. If he hadn't stumbled across it, he never would've noticed.

The few large bones that remained with the animal's spine and skull were massive and cracked because of its obvious fall from the top of the hill. The bones were bleached pure white from years of scavenging and sunshine. He didn't know how many decades the skeleton had been there, but could tell that it had been quite a while.

When he strapped the head to his backpack, Daniel nearly lost his balance. The longhorn skull sported a nearly six-foot span of perfectly-curved horns, neatly preserved by the dry sand of the creek bed. It had been heavy on his back as he'd hiked to his truck, but he was able to sell it to a local collector for over a thousand dollars.

Daniel later learned that the last group of longhorn cattle to travel across that land had been a herd of escapees from the railroad pens at Belle Fourche, almost a hundred miles away. That was before barbed wire divided the land. It was before the end of the Civil War and before statehood for South Dakota.

That sort of occasional profit, along with the adventure of solving a centuries-old mystery, was enough to keep Daniel going when it seemed like predator hunting was a lousy way to make a living.

Chapter Three

Sometimes, clients insisted on coming with him. Whether it was the fact that Daniel was a young man that they thought may require supervision, or if it was out of sheer boredom that often beset even the most hardworking farmer between planting and harvest, Daniel didn't know. Truthfully, it didn't matter to him what their motives were. He needed all of the word-of-mouth advertising he could get, and there was no better way to garner that praise than to take someone along to watch him work.

There was a wheat farmer in eastern Montana who'd insisted on lugging his ancient deer rifle along. He'd tried and come up short in an effort to eradicate the badgers that were tearing up his expansive fields. Given free rein, badgers dug several holes in the most inconvenient places imaginable. This resulted in a lot of costly repair work on the man's expensive combines and harvesting equipment.

Daniel knew the old man had good intentions and he didn't protest, but he also knew that the farmer's .30-30 would be ineffective medicine for a badger in this terrain. Sure, the bullet would do the trick, but with iron sights, the man would never get close enough to prove it.

Daniel's choice for small to mid-sized varmints, a .22-250 that he mated to a tactical-style turret scope, would easily reach out to four hundred yards, and the number nearly doubled with no crosswind.

When the old man asked why Daniel hadn't brought a "real" gun, his simple reply was dropping to the prone position on top of a rise. He handed his binoculars to the farmer, then proceeded to pick off a badger sauntering up an adjacent hill from nearly half a mile away.

"My goodness!" the man exclaimed. The binoculars were shaking as he handed them back to Daniel.

For the next three days Daniel hunted on his own, and when he left there were no more badgers on the property. By the time he was done on that farm, there were three more local farmers who were interested in hiring him. They had heard from their neighbor about "the Dakota kid who can shoot like nobody else."

That evening Daniel went from being a scavenger, finding horns and stretching pelts, to being a hired gun.

Later, in northern Missouri, he'd been hired by a small-town poultry farmer to take care of a cagey predator that had been getting into the long, low barns and making off with dozens of his chickens every night. Even though the farm raised thousands of birds at a time, his slim profit margin meant that every single chicken was valuable.

"I think there's just one coyote—I've only ever seen one anyways—but he is a wily," the man said. "I've tried trapping the furry rascal in one barn, but it's like he's got a sixth sense. He just goes to the next barn, then the next one."

"It sounds to me like you've got a pack of coyotes working your property. They're taking turns," Daniel replied. "It's just that you've only ever seen one, the lead dog of the pack."

"Well, son, it could be. I hope you get every last one of them," the farmer said. "They're eatin' me out of house and home!"

The chicken farmer had heard of Daniel's

exploits up on the prairie, where his wife's second cousin ran a feed store. Around a community coffee pot that attracted farmers like flies to a candied apple, the shopkeeper listened as several local ranchers bragged about Daniel, who had solved their varmint problem. The man told his relative in Missouri, who wisely called Daniel after he failed to kill the problem animal on his own.

One week after their initial meeting, Daniel collected payment and showed the farmer thirteen fresh coyote pelts on the tailgate of his pickup truck.

Those jobs had been relatively easy. The hardest part had simply been getting his name on the lips of those who could help promote him.

Chapter Four

With plenty of offers, Daniel was able to raise his prices. Now, he charged a flat fee per animal, plus an allowance for mileage travelled and any license expenses. He watched the fur market diligently, and, when it was profitable to do so, he also negotiated the right to any pelts.

Predator hunting the way Daniel did it— immersing himself in a landscape and melding with it until the job was done—was a niche market. There were plenty of hunters and trappers around, particularly in the west, but most of them were hobbyists who couldn't afford to dedicate the time and energy required to travel great distances, or to bed down in the dirt for days on end like Daniel often did.

Whenever possible, he made a point of checking in with local law enforcement before starting a job in their jurisdiction. It was a common courtesy that they appreciated, and it usually garnered him a hassle-free hunt in the area. Police officers, sheriffs, and game wardens usually had their fingers on the pulse of an area as well, which meant that they might have some information that could help him accomplish his mission.

Daniel had earned a reputation as someone who paid strict attention to detail, who didn't damage property or trespass, and who got results. Every job he took was bid as "until completion," which was a promise to the landowner and to himself. Failure was not an option.

He hadn't run across another person who took his approach. Daniel's services were in demand by those who wanted a predator problem solved, not simply addressed.

His current job was in northwestern Wyoming. Several months earlier, a large hospitality corporation named Hanco Ventures had broken ground on a new ski resort. After cutting through a mountain of red tape, arranging land exchanges with the government, buying out local mining interests, and paying off enough politicians to push the project through a contentious public comment period, the Highland Peak resort was given the green light to start construction.

Hanco immediately deployed the first crews to start infrastructure improvements at the base of the mountain. For a ski town that would rival Aspen, Taos, and nearby Jackson, that meant a complete renovation of the electrical, sewer, water, and transportation services to the area. Massive earthmovers came rumbling up the narrow canyon road on semi-trucks with "Wide Load" placards, and the ground was soon devoid of trees and natural vegetation. Pipelines and conduit were laid beneath the soil. Asphalt and gravel took the place of bunchgrass and sagebrush.

After the groundwork had been finished and the utilities had been brought on line, contractors from all over the country descended on the base area. They were tasked with building the structures required to operate a world-class ski resort. Everything from multi-level concrete parking ramps to a high-speed gondola had to be hauled up the canyon road and constructed.

Further up the mountain, smaller crews came in to erect "ski-in/ski-out" condominiums around the edges of the slopes. Row after row of timber-framed buildings began to rise toward the clear springtime sky in short order. Things were progressing ahead of schedule, and it looked as if

Highland Peak would open in time for the coming ski season. That was when the problem began.

At first, workers were unnerved to see paw prints around their construction trailers and equipment. The high-steel crew working on the base area improvements was made up of men who hailed from the downtown St. Louis area. They knew very little about the mountains or the wildlife that resided there, but their company's bid had been the cheapest; they were transplanted to the mountains of Wyoming immediately.

Rows of temporary housing trailers occupied one corner of the construction staging area, beside stockpiles of steel, lumber, and wire. There were also trailers that provided food, shower facilities, and medical care. For men who were away from their homes, having a comfortable bed and a hot meal each night made the sting of loneliness a little less severe.

Many of the workers on the project were happy to have the job—any job. Their prospects for employment back in the city were slim due to a failing local economy and a lack of seniority. Some were just starting their careers in construction. Others had a run-in with the law and needed a fresh start. For them, the Highland Peak project was just what they needed.

Hanco had little time for background checks or seniority. Rather, it needed warm bodies and strong backs to get the resort up and running as soon as possible. The investors in the Highland Peak project were anxious to see a return on their money, and the company acted accordingly. As long as the work got done, the men were left alone.

Some of the workers, particularly the younger crew members, had never been out of their home cities before this project. It was an adventure for them, an opportunity to see a different part of the country and to make a very good wage while they did. They worked six days a week for twelve hours a day.

The paw prints were there, a daily reminder to everyone on the site that they were far out of their element.

Chapter Five

A month into the project, nearly everyone had lost interest in whatever was prowling around the site at night. Workers grew increasingly bold, venturing into the woods rather than using the portable toilets provided. Sack lunches from the cafeteria trailer were taken up the slope and enjoyed on sunny rock outcroppings. Men with cell phones, who had initially been frustrated by the lack of reception at the base, took advantage of their day off to hike up the mountain where they could get service. At the summit, several industrious workers had constructed a table and chairs out of logs. The seating area was a favorite destination for the older men in the crew, who hiked up every week like clockwork to call their wives and children back in the city.

State-of-the-art ski lifts were due to be installed all over the resort at the end of summer. Concrete crews began forming and pouring foundations for the massive steel poles at escalating distances up the mountainsides. For weeks, the only signs that anything was amiss were the paw prints in the dirt each morning. Everything else seemed to be perfect. Men were simply working hard on a jobsite like they would anywhere else.

The first attack took place on a lazy afternoon in the middle of June. A twenty-five-year-old concrete worker, Nathaniel Washington, was eating his sack lunch just a few hundred yards up the first slope, inside a dense stand of pines that bordered the planned ski run. He sat on a small rock at the base of a much taller one and stared out contentedly at the valley below him.

His work day was halfway done, and he was happy to be in such a beautiful place. Nathaniel liked Wyoming: it was quiet and peaceful. *A man could make a decent life here,* he thought.

Tomorrow was his day off, and he looked forward to hiking up the mountain so he could call his girlfriend. In a few weeks, when the concrete pole bases had all been poured, his time in Wyoming would be over. He would head back to St. Louis with a full bank account.

He wanted to go home and marry his girl, then move back out west. She'd love it out here, with the stars and the trees. Maybe he'd start his own concrete business in Highland Peak.

He bent down to pour some coffee from his thermos and it wound up being his last move. When Nathaniel didn't show up to work that afternoon, his friends wondered what had happened. That night, when he didn't take his regular seat in the dining hall, they alerted the foreman. A man missing work for the afternoon was something that happened occasionally, but a man missing a meal? That didn't happen without good reason.

Two days later, deputies from the local sheriff's office found his body by following the squawking sounds of an excited group of magpies. Nathaniel's remains were half eaten and hidden behind a downed tree. The cause of death was as clear as day: four deep slash marks across the front of his neck, too perfect and uniform to have been caused by scavenging birds, along with four puncture wounds on the top of his spine. A mountain lion had ambushed him.

The workers were immediately put through a day-long course in mountain lion safety. Hanco hired two highly educated national experts to come to Wyoming and instruct the laborers on the habits of big feline predators. The experts, who both held multiple degrees from prestigious institutions, had a lot of insight into what may have provoked the cat into attacking Nathaniel.

"The cat may have been sick," one of the experts remarked. "Often, ailing felines will abandon their instinctive fear of bipedal creatures because they're desperate for an easy meal."

"In my opinion, the most likely cause for this particular attack is a decline in the deer population," the other professional said. "Deer comprise the majority of a mountain lion's diet. Recently, we've seen a strain of infection in mule deer in this area that has caused the population to dwindle."

Workers were encouraged to stay close to camp and to travel in pairs. Every foreman was outfitted with a semi-automatic 9 mm pistol, and each construction trailer housed a pair of 12-gauge shotguns that could be used to deter a big cat if one was seen. This seemed to be a legitimate plan—allowing those who were in danger to defend themselves, but it had one big problem: most of the workers had never fired a gun.

Since construction began in April, six lion attacks had left Nathaniel Washington and three other men dead. Another man, the fifth victim, escaped death but was permanently disabled. Each of the attacks had been an unlikely scenario where no amount of preparation would've been sufficient. One had been in an open meadow, and another had been just inside the back doors of a steel shipping container. The most egregious attack was on a bulldozer operator while he sat on his machine—with the diesel engine running. It was clear that the cat, or cats, was not afraid of humans.

The only man who escaped unharmed told his wife, co-workers, and the newspaper reporters that it was the most terrifying experience of his life. He avoided serious injury by stuffing his hand and arm as far down the cat's throat as possible—a trick he'd learned as a boy with a frisky Rottweiler around the house.

After the man's story hit the internet and went viral, it made national headlines. Pundits and activists for both the workers and the mountain lions began to protest Hanco for their practices. Representatives from the country's largest labor union appeared out of nowhere and quickly organized the site, then called for a strike. There was no way the project could move forward. Work on Highland Peak ground to a halt on the nineteenth of September.

That's when Daniel got the call.

Chapter Six

The corporation's public-affairs officer, Gregory Ludlow, was a rosy-cheeked thirty-something who looked like he'd just come from a mountaineering store. His wardrobe was made up of name-brand clothing that didn't quite fit him, and his high-end hiking boots showed no signs of scuffing or wear. When they met to discuss Hanco's mountain lion problem at a small diner in Jackson Hole, Daniel could immediately tell that Ludlow was not as avid an outdoorsman as he tried to portray.

"Mr. Ludlow," Daniel started after they'd placed their orders and taken seats at a table.

"Please, call me Greg," Ludlow cut him off. "Mr. Ludlow was my dad," the company man said with a smile. His polished demeanor and thick black glasses were at odds with the drab canvas jacket he wore.

"Okay, Greg," Daniel replied. "Can you tell me what we're dealing with?"

"Well, not exactly. I'll take you up to the jobsite and let you know the circumstances of each attack," Greg replied. "But I don't know how much I can help you with planning your hunt." His voice turned low, as if in apology. "I just shipped in here from our headquarters in Houston last week, and I've only had a little bit of time to look around the mountain."

Daniel had seen Greg's face on television the night before. The man had been sent to Jackson Hole as a mouthpiece for the company to deal with the press.

"Forgive me for saying this, Greg, but you don't strike me as the mountaineering type," Daniel posed, his eyes looking toward the pretty girl who was delivering their coffee order. She had a familiar look, he thought. Pretty auburn hair and green eyes.

His mind quickly wandered back to memories of an earlier hunt, where he'd come across a mixed-up city girl in the mountains of Montana and had kept her safe. He and Marissa had bonded over the course of the hunt, alone in the backcountry, and had carried the relationship back to North Dakota when the job was finished. She was beautiful, and Daniel had fallen hard for the first time in his life. Things had gone smoothly, and they spoke of their life together on several occasions. Then she disappeared without a trace. For months, he found no sign of her.

With the nature of his work, Daniel spent many hours behind the wheel of his truck. It gave him ample time to think about the future. Unfortunately, it gave him plenty of time to mull over the past, too. He replayed the entirety of his relationship with Marissa every time the road stretched out before him. Still, he could find no answer to his question: *Why had she left him?*

Daniel was pulled back from his daydream when Greg spoke again.

"Truthfully, it's been a long time since I was out in the mountains," he said. "I used to go fly fishing with my grandpa down in Colorado. Every summer, we'd spend a few weeks living out of an old wall tent at different trailheads. It was my favorite thing to do."

Greg's eyes wandered as he spoke, but came back to meet Daniel's. "Hanco sent me up here because I'm the youngest representative we've got." His face fell. "I'm supposed to fit in with the locals and show that the company cares."

"What do you mean?" Daniel asked.

"I mean that we're a big company full of rich old men who don't look like they empathize with the plight of the working man. If one of our board members was up here talking to the press, we'd get crucified in the media. They'd go on and on about how we're putting profit over workers' safety, or how we're pillaging the landscape in pursuit of the almighty dollar." Suddenly, his eyes danced with amusement. "I'm the young, understanding, caring, forward-thinking, *remarkably handsome* face of the company!" Greg's face broke into a wide grin.

They finished their coffee and drove to Highland Peak, which looked like a post-apocalyptic ghost town. There were rows of heavy machines sitting idly by, waiting to be restarted. The barracks were empty. No diesel generators hummed, no lights flickered. No life was apparent on the site.

One trailer sat perpendicular to the rest, and Greg pulled his shiny rental SUV up near the door. Daniel wheeled his trusty pickup truck—with its rusted wheel wells and oversized tires—into the spot next to it. The two trucks were a fair representation of the two drivers. Both were capable. Both had their strong suits. One would look good on camera. The other could survive in the mud.

Inside the trailer, a map of the area had been tacked up on the back wall. On a tall table below the map, paperwork was piled high. Notes were pinned everywhere. On the map, six red push pins denoted the six mountain lion attacks. Greg walked Daniel through each occurrence, then tried to answer any questions Daniel had. After that, the two sat down at a desk and went through the contract Hanco's lawyers had sent along with Greg. The main point in all the legalese was: if Daniel got killed, it wasn't Hanco's fault.

Daniel's reputation had grown to the point that he no longer had to go looking for work; *it* found *him*. He learned to charge what he was worth: the final contract he signed with Hanco Ventures paid him an initial fee of ten thousand dollars, plus mileage, incidental expenses, and a whopping five thousand dollars per cat killed. It had the potential to be Daniel's biggest pay day yet.

Greg had one special request for Daniel: the members of Hanco Ventures' board of directors wanted one mountain lion delivered to a local taxidermist for a stuffed display in their Houston office. All other pelts were his to keep. Mountain lion furs were not a hot commodity on the garment market, but many taxidermists would gladly buy hides if they were properly fleshed and salted, a technique used to preserve them. Much like trophy bucks and bulls, a nice full-body cat mount would sell through an interior decorator for plenty of money.

Corporate America, Daniel thought. He wondered what his life might've been like if he'd chosen a more typical career path—like Greg.

Daniel had never considered being a part of the nine-to-five workforce, even as a youth. From an early age, he knew that the outdoors were where he would make his living. Early career considerations had ranged from farming, like his grandparents had done, to roughnecking in the Bakken oil patch, as a few of his cousins were currently doing. The thought of sitting in an office made him itch.

Instead, Daniel made money doing the thing he loved. Some days were miserable and some were fantastic, but it was rarely dull. Almost everything he did was dangerous, but that's what made it so exciting.

Chapter Seven

It was well into the afternoon when Greg finally departed back to Jackson Hole. They only spent a short time together, but Daniel felt better after meeting him. It was nice to know that someone had his back, should things take a wrong turn.

"Well, I'd better head back to deal with the latest round of activist nutjobs and bloggers," Greg said, stepping toward the door of the trailer. "Make sure you call me if there's anything I can do to help."

"I will, Greg. Thanks," Daniel said, extending his hand. "I'll be up on the mountain for quite a while now, but I'll let you know if I get into Jackson."

The men shook hands and Greg exited. Daniel heard his tires clicking across the gravel parking lot, the hum of the SUV's big motor fading soon after. For the foreseeable future, it was just him and the mountain.

The area he was hunting was a massive piece of property. Early brochures for Highland Peak had claimed that the resort would have "over 5,000 skiable acres." That figure played well with Hanco's qualified investors, who were eager to be a part of something so grand. In reality, the company had staked out twenty contiguous sections of terrain for a total of nearly thirteen thousand acres. It was the sort of land grab that railroads had made famous over a century earlier, when the west was being settled. Whatever went on around Highland Peak in the future, the money would go through Hanco's hands first.

Getting back into the hills was Daniel's first priority. Even though several of the attacks had occurred close to the base area, he reasoned that a predator went to where the prey lived. Now that the construction area was deserted, there was very little chance that a cat would be nearby. He intended to go deep into the mountains where deer and other species were abundant.

He had access to Hanco's fleet of ATVs and snowmobiles, but did not intend to use them. True, the cats had proven to be unaffected by engine noise and exhaust fumes, but the other wildlife had not. If he was going to look for mountain lions by looking for their prey, he couldn't risk spooking them. Instead, he would hike up slowly and quietly, as if he were on any other big game hunt.

With a final look around the jobsite trailer, Daniel stepped outside and closed the door behind him. He made a point of leaving one of the lights on inside, and opened a tattered window blind facing the ski hill. If he had to get down the mountain in the dark during the hunt, he hoped this light would be a beacon to navigate toward.

Outside, he climbed into the bed of his truck and began piecing together his tool kit for the hunt. Beneath the fiberglass topper, all the gear he needed was stowed in plastic storage tubs. His external-frame backpack soon pressed tightly at the seams as he added clothing from one tub and cooking gear from another. A small tent got strapped on top, and a variable-power spotting scope was tucked into a padded side pocket. Everything had its own place, like a carpenter's tools in a toolbelt.

With his camping gear set, Daniel turned his attention to outfitting himself. His jeans and cowboy boots were replaced by a light pair of mountaineering pants and a set of stiff hunting lace-ups. Next, he made sure to put a brand-new butane lighter in each hip pocket. Lastly, he threaded a holster onto his belt and dropped in a big-bore revolver.

Even though this hunt was for mountain lions, Daniel wore the pistol as a precaution against bears. There were grizzly bears and black bears in this part of the country, and being prepared for an attack was just an extra form of insurance. It was unlikely that the weapon would see use—or even come out of its holster—but it gave Daniel a sense of security. On a backcountry hunt, anything could happen. He'd used the pistol in self-defense before.

Daniel shouldered into his backpack and closed the truck topper, then grabbed his primary weapon, a semi-automatic rifle chambered for .223. The gun was a short-barreled unit with a holographic sight mounted in place of a scope. Quick follow-up shots were essential in cat country, and this rig fit the bill. The sight was almost unnoticeable when shooting instinctively at close range, but was more accurate than standard iron sights at long range.

With nothing left for him at the base area, Daniel stepped out eagerly for the first slope, anxious to get to the center of the parcel. He planned to set up camp in a drainage nearly three miles away from the base, which would've been an easy walk without the mountains rising up before him. Following one of the many overgrown trails that Hanco's bulldozers had carved into the landscape earlier that summer, he felt the familiar rush of adrenaline that always carried him forward on his hunts. There was no certainty in the mountains, but there was always adventure. He quickened his pace and headed right for whatever lay ahead.

Chapter Eight

All around him, the landscape breathed out warmly in the late afternoon sunshine. When he reached the top of the first tall pitch, Daniel saw the rough logs of the workers' picnic spot. He stopped for a moment to consider his next step. Setting up his spotting scope, he took in the country around him. In a bare meadow to the west, he could see stakes and faded pink ribbons marking the future site of a ski lift base unit. To the north, a tall mountain rose out of the aspen bottoms and went up like a spire into the stratosphere. This mountain had been invisible from the base area, but that didn't surprise

Daniel. Often, the difference of a few feet changed one's perspective enough that he could see a lot of new country. Mountain views were different with every step.

Consulting his topographic map, Daniel concluded that his favored campsite lay just over the western shoulder of the looming mountain. With daylight waning, he couldn't afford to waste any more time. He didn't want to be setting up his camp in the dark—not in dangerous cat country. Quickly, Daniel marched toward his intended spot. It was difficult walking on uneven terrain, made only slightly more comfortable when he struck a game trail.

In the last hint of direct sunlight over the distant western peaks, Daniel dropped off a ridge and down into his campsite. The grassy floor of the drainage was soggy with runoff, even this late in the year. A small rocky bench, only twenty yards across, rose from the creek bottom. It was roughly shaped like a rectangle, and the top of it was mostly bare rock. One spot, however, was filled with pine duff and dirt, which would provide decent insulation and relative comfort for someone sleeping on the ground. The plateau was nearly level, and Daniel decided to set up his tent here with the flap—and his feet—pointed slightly downhill.

It was nearly pitch-black outside by the time he got his camp set up. The first thing he did was gather what nearby wood he could to build a fire. Luckily, a standing dead lodgepole pine was just inside the edge of the forest behind his camp. This tree would supply him with plenty of firewood for the night. Tomorrow he would have to find a few more dry, dead trees around the small meadow to keep his fire going in the days to come.

After the fire was started and burning steadily, he unfolded a small tarp on the rocks, then set up his tent. It was something he'd done so often, the poles and fabric seemed to assemble themselves. His sleeping bag and pad were unrolled inside soon after.

With a small panful of water from the trickling stream in front of him, he set a pot of water to boiling for a dinner of freeze-dried beef stew. Also, he mixed a cup of instant apple cider. As his bagged dinner sat in front of him on a rock, sealed up to steep for a few minutes before eating, he leaned back against his pack and cradled the warm drink in his hands.

The very last of a clear night's alpenglow showed itself on the high peak above him. Daniel scanned the face of the mountain, looking at it with a hunter's eye. He checked boxes of an imaginary list in his mind.

Where did the water run? Where was it too steep to walk? What lived up there and where? Would it take him an hour or a day to climb it?

All of these questions would be answered in the next few days, he knew.

As the light finally faded, stars began to appear on either side of the peak. It was only by the lack of starlight that he knew where the mountain blocked his view to the heavens. Tomorrow morning's sunrise would come late. The peak would block any warming rays until long after the animals, and Daniel, had started their day.

He woke up early the next morning, as he always did in the hills. A general dampness hung in the air around his site and inside his tent. Drops of condensation clung to the inside walls of his shelter, the remnants of his warm breath against a chilly fabric throughout the night.

When he climbed out of the flap and into the clearing, Daniel instinctively scanned the small meadow for game. It was just barely light enough to see the far edge of the creek.

Back in Mandan, whitetail hunters referred to this time of day as the "magic hour," when deer were still moving and feeding before heading back to their sanctuaries to pass the daylight hours with their eyes closed. It was a perfect time for dedicated hunters to catch deer with their guard down.

This morning in Wyoming, the magic hour proved to be an interstate measure. There, on the far side of the clearing, two mule deer does and their fawns browsed contentedly on brush that grew above the creek. Daniel found his binoculars and settled down to watch for a while.

When the deer had gone, their white rumps disappearing into the timber completely, Daniel kindled a small fire and set some water to boiling. Coffee and a packet of instant oatmeal would sustain him until he could make use of what the mountain had to offer. He carried a slingshot with him on most alpine hunts and hoped to dine on either grouse or rabbit tonight. The first thing on his mind, however, was surveying the country. Lion hunting was far more important than killing his dinner.

Chapter Nine

Two hours later, Daniel had finally reached the sunlight. He went northwest out of camp and headed the only way he could—uphill. Careful of his steps and of the wind direction, he soon came to the edge of a saddle, hidden halfway up the mammoth mountain. Before plunging headlong into the warming rays, though, he scanned the ground ahead of him. For the second time that morning, he spotted game before it spotted him.

Out in the middle of the clearing, a large bull Shiras moose stood black against the light brown grass. Daniel brought his binoculars up and examined the animal. From head to toe, it was built for survival in the harshest of climates. Strands of velvet hung from its blood-stained antlers, each palmated side resembling a jagged canoe paddle. The massive animal would make any moose hunter's trophy room look a lot better.

Content to sit and watch, Daniel backed up to a tree and settled down on his haunches. Moose were often aggressive during the breeding season, and the last thing he wanted was fourteen hundred pounds of rut-crazed bull chasing him through the trees. There was no way around the moose except for retracing his steps, and Daniel had no intention of giving up any elevation. He would wait—and watch—until the bull left.

Suddenly, a piercing bugle came out of the woods behind the moose, across the clearing. Elk were also rutting this time of year. Like hormone-crazed teenagers, both species—during the breeding season—would often act in ways that were unwise. Many bull elk were killed every autumn by bowhunters doing their best impersonation of a cow elk.

Just after the bugle, a ruckus broke out in the trees behind the moose. It sounded like a pair of bull elk were pummeling one another, sparring with their antlers for the right to mate. Something about the sound was odd to Daniel, though. He'd witnessed elk fighting with one another many times, and had never heard anything other than the clatter of antlers crashing together when the fight was on. This time, he heard an odd hissing noise amid the sounds of scraping hooves and rustling leaves.

The bull moose decided that this battle didn't concern him, and he jogged away with remarkable grace. With the threat of being discovered now gone, Daniel eased into the clearing and closer to the fight, which was escalating. When he was within about forty yards of the thrashing trees and undergrowth that signaled where the altercation was taking place, Daniel finally figured out what the strange hissing noise was.

It must be a mountain lion, he reasoned. *I've never heard of a mountain lion taking on a bull elk!*

Suddenly, as if his thought process had been live-streamed to the two combatants, he heard a deep, rumbling scream come from the trees. The bull elk and a massive cat wrestled their way out of the brush and right toward Daniel.

Instinctively, Daniel reached to his hip and unsnapped the thumb-break on his holster. If they got any closer, he would make a run for it. And if the cat got clear, he would take a shot.

The two fighting animals were a mess. Bleeding from claw marks on its shoulder and rump, the bull had clearly been taken by surprise.

Getting the upper hand hadn't been enough. The cat was now pinned beneath the bull's antlers, and was being pushed along the ground like snow before a plow. Each bump in the terrain elicited a snarl from the lion, as the elk's sharp tines pushed deeper into its body.

Time seemed to stand still as the battle raged. Daniel could see the bull's heaving sides and quaking muscles as it pushed to survive. Likewise, he heard the cat's snarl come and go, and saw its bared claws reaching with everything it had, trying to slash the bull and end the ride. It was one of the rawest examples of nature's ferocity that Daniel had ever seen.

Just when it seemed that the lion was about to perish, the bull stumbled and lurched to one side, giving the cat a small window to escape. The mountain lion expertly twisted its body around and leapt away, then wheeled toward the elk again. Back on its feet, the bull lowered its head and waited. Daniel could tell that if the fight didn't end soon, the bull would die of exhaustion and from its open wounds, which were pouring blood and staining its muted brown hide a bright crimson.

The lion made one final charge, leaping from its position and heading right for the elk's neck. At the last minute, the bull lifted its head and ran a sharp brow tine right through the lion's front shoulder. The cat howled in pain and recoiled before fully coming to rest on the elk's head. With a last-ditch effort, the bull spun and flung the lion over its shoulder and onto a rock.

For a moment, neither animal moved. Daniel could see the lion lying where it had landed. Its sides were rising and falling in rapid succession. The bull, exhausted, stood on quivering legs and watched. Slowly, Daniel eased his pistol out of its holster. He could hardly grasp the weapon because he was shaking so severely, and after several attempts to level his sights on the cat, he gave up. The adrenaline of being so close to something so visceral overtook him. He lowered his pistol in defeat, unable to compose himself enough to make the shot.

The lion stirred, then pulled its feet beneath it. With a low snarl and an almost-sarcastic look over its shoulder at the bull, it rose on three legs and limped off. Where it laid, a large pool of dark blood covered the granite.

Daniel watched the cat slink away and disappear, then turned his head to look at the bull. It was still standing in a defensive posture, legs locked, head low. Its left ear was torn in two from the fight, but the appendage still seemed to follow the cat's soft footsteps as it strode away. Nearly a minute after Daniel had lost sight of the cat, the bull seemed satisfied that it was no longer in danger.

Moving out into the clearing on stiff legs, well away from any trees or rocks that might hide a return attack from the lion, the bull collapsed into the grass. Just when he thought that the elk might've found its own gravesite, Daniel saw the proud animal roll onto its belly, tilt its head back, and let out a defiant bugle.

He'll be alright, Daniel decided.

Chapter Ten

Back at his camp that evening, Daniel mulled over the events of the day. The battle between the elk and the lion had etched itself firmly in his mind, and he replayed it several times while he went about preparing dinner.

If that cat was bold enough to take on a bull elk, it must be one of the lions responsible for attacking the construction workers, he surmised.

Something else about his day on the mountain bothered him, though. Three hours after witnessing the battle, he managed to reach the summit of the big peak. He purposely avoided following the injured lion's trail, because few things were more dangerous than a wounded predator.

Daniel had taken a circuitous route to the highest point in the land, the windswept mountaintop devoid of anything but rocks and a few low-slung mahogany bushes. There was no good reason for any living thing to spend time up there. After a long time glassing the surrounding country he headed back down the hill, retracing his steps from the way up.

Two hundred yards down the slope, Daniel came across something disturbing. There, in a tiny patch of lingering snow he'd crossed earlier, his boot prints were clearly visible. Instead of just the outline of his soles, though, a distinct lion track was now evident. And where the snow was deep enough, bright red blood stained the depressions. A startling thought occurred to him: *the wounded cat had followed him up the mountain.*

Daniel froze, not sure of himself for the second time that day. He looked around quickly, trying in vain to find more tracks.

The cat had been there, that much he was sure of. But where had it gone from there? And why had it stalked him up the mountain?

He mulled the questions over back at camp. All afternoon, he still-hunted his way down the mountain. Checking his back trail every few steps grated on his nerves, exhausting him mentally. By the time he got back to camp, every sound in the woods made him jump. He was as nervous as a grasshopper on a chicken farm.

If that cat decided to stalk me all over the mountain, even though it was injured, what else was it capable of? Daniel wondered. *Would it be scared of a fire? A tent?*

He kindled a blaze and stoked it as fast as it would take fuel. Soon, he had a large display of flame and smoke out in front of the tent. Finally, as the sun disappeared and darkness slowly overtook his meadow, Daniel's nerves began to settle. His jumpiness from the afternoon was fading, and he regained his composure.

There was something about a campfire that always calmed Daniel down and gave him peace of mind. He came to realize that, when something needed to be figured out, there was no better place for him to think.

Many Friday nights during high school, he'd avoided going to field parties with his classmates. Instead of going out, Daniel took up a familiar post in his parents' backyard. That was where he planned his hunts. It was also where he sifted through his future plans—where he would go, if he would attend college, and how he would make money.

Beside the fire was where Daniel had first considered making his living hunting wild, sometimes dangerous animals. Armed with an empty notebook and a stubby lumber pencil, he hammered out a business plan in the orange glow of burning branches. When he had a rough idea of how things would go, he took the plan to a few local men he knew who ran good businesses. Their input had helped him straighten out the crooked path between a wild idea and a viable business.

More recently, as he made his way around the country completing difficult jobs, Daniel found himself building fires nearly every night so he could ponder a much more personal issue— Marissa.

He tried to make sense of the situation. Why did she leave? Everything seemed fine between them the last time they spoke, before he left for a job in Utah. They hadn't fought or had a cross word between them. She was happy to see him off with a kiss and a lunch for the road.

Marissa's sudden disappearance came as a

total surprise. When he returned to Mandan after the job, he stopped in at the diner where she worked as a waitress. Johnny, the longtime cook, looked at him cautiously and shook his head. Marissa wasn't at work, he said. She hadn't been for nearly a week.

When he went to her apartment, a small garage attic downtown, Daniel was startled to see a "For Rent" sign in the window. The landlord said Marissa had left town in the middle of the night six days before. She hadn't left word for him, either.

Now, in the firelight, Daniel laid everything out in order. He knew she was gone, and the way she left made it clear that he wasn't supposed to find her. It was sour medicine but that was the truth. Marissa, for whatever reason, didn't want to be his girl anymore.

The thoughts that had tormented him in every spare moment came rushing forth. Had she been lying to him the whole time they were together? Or, had she simply gotten carried away? Was their relationship a vacation for her, something useful for a time, but not permanent? Had he been her retreat from something bigger until it came time for her to get back to her real life?

Mulling these things over in his mind, Daniel came to the conclusion that answers to his questions may never come. Marissa was gone, and she wasn't coming back. Whatever he thought they had together was over now, and he had to move on.

The fire had nearly died when Daniel forced himself up from the ground next to the embers. There was moisture on his cheeks. It wasn't the first time he'd shed tears over Marissa, but he hoped it would be the last. Her hold on him was unhealthy and could compromise his judgment if he let it. In the mountains, that could be deadly.

Pushing aside the sad thoughts, Daniel got back to work. He quickly made a meal of prepackaged noodles, then settled into his sleeping bag for what promised to be a fitful night of sleep with his pistol in his hand.

The last thing that crossed his mind before he shut his eyes was a declaration:

I'm going to take care of this—all this garbage going on in my head, and I'm going to kill this mountain lion before it kills me.

Chapter Eleven

The squawk of a Canadian jay on his tent pole was the first thing Daniel heard the next morning. In his unfocused state the night before, he forgot to wash out his dishes. When he emerged from the tent, two puffy gray camp robbers sat on his various utensils that he left lying by the smoldering fire, eyeing him warily.

He made it through the night safely. Quietly, he looked up toward the mountaintop and took a moment to count his blessings.

After breakfast, Daniel checked his weapons to make sure they were in working order, then headed back up the mountain to where the fight had taken place. He needed to follow the blood trail of the wounded cat to see if he could figure out what it was up to. If the lion had spotted him by chance as he climbed the mountain, then followed out of curiosity, that was one thing. But if—as he suspected—the lion had a taste for humans and had seen him after the fight and stalked him up the mountain, that was another thing entirely.

It didn't surprise him to find the bull elk still nearby when he got to the saddle. The animal spooked from its bed when Daniel entered the open meadow, clearly still jumpy from the battle it had taken part in the day before. As it departed through the trees, Daniel could see the dark claw marks on its hindquarter. However long it lived, that bull would carry the scars of its dance with death.

Above the saddle, Daniel picked up the cat's

trail and followed it easily until it met his own tracks from the day before. The cat had stayed remarkably close to him for most of the journey, its paw prints only a few yards uphill from Daniel's boot marks most of the way. Given the time it took him to glass and return down the mountain, Daniel came to a conclusion: the cat had followed him by sight alone. It watched and prowled along with him until the very top of the mountain.

I would've never known what hit me if that lion had decided to attack, Daniel thought. *I've got to be more observant from here on out.*

One thing that he hoped to capitalize on was the lion's fear of open country. It was almost like the cat knew that, if given the opportunity, Daniel would level his sights on it and the game would be over. Right at the tree line, where he first noticed the cat's tracks in his own the day before, he could now clearly see what had occurred.

It looked like the cat had vanished, but in reality, it had simply taken up an ambush location in a tree. Daniel could see the marks from its razor-sharp claws on a leaning tree's trunk, and found a small tuft of tan fur snagged on a branch. On the downhill side of the tree, twenty yards past the trunk, Daniel found a mark in the snow where the lion had given up its vigil and leapt down.

Perhaps it had grown tired of waiting, or perhaps the cat's wounds were bothering it. Either way, Daniel was lucky. The cat had been all set to spring on him when he returned from glassing. If the cat had been there, he would've wound up like the other workers on the mountain: dead.

There was no sign of the animal now, though. Daniel reasoned that it must have gone in search of easier prey. Rabbits abounded in the creek bottoms, and would be a particularly easy meal for a predator as talented as this cat. Watching his backtrail, Daniel descended from the peak again, this time on the opposite side. He wound his way down the mountain on a network of game trails and was nearly back to the saddle when he heard the telltale sound of a fawn bleating.

Quickly, Daniel rushed to the source of the noise. Coming around a final stand of trees, he found himself on the edge of a vertical rock face, and the bottom was several hundred feet down. One more step and he'd have been in freefall.

Chapter Twelve

There, on top of the box canyon wall, Daniel saw a grisly scene playing out below. A mountain lion and her two yearling kittens were busy picking apart a mule deer doe and her fawn. The mother cat had performed her task efficiently on the doe, and the deer was nearly still by the time Daniel trained his binoculars on it.

The kittens, identifiable as such by their smaller size and slightly discolored lower leg fur, traded off between killing the fawn and tackling one another. It was a method of training for the young lions, Daniel knew from his study on the species. While it was difficult to watch the fawn struggling, it was a necessary part of the development process for the cats. They would be out on their own before too long. The deer fawn's eerie, sad bleating soon ceased, and the three cats settled in to fill their bellies.

From his position, Daniel could easily take out the mother cat with a single shot from his rifle. At around a hundred yards, there was no question about his accuracy. It would be an easy way for him to show Hanco that he could get results—but he didn't raise his weapon.

Seeing the cat and her kittens in their natural habitat, without bulldozers or concrete or ski lifts, brought Daniel's mind back to the true purpose of his mission. He wasn't there to kill every cat on the mountain, he was there to kill the cats that were killing people. These mountain lions were simply wild things interacting in a wild world, untouched by humans. They were not the cats he was hired to eliminate.

Daniel watched for a few more minutes as the lions dismantled their prey, then he backed away from his vantage point and headed back to the saddle. It was well after lunch time and he was hungry. He decided to check a likely ridge for grouse.

Heading south toward the log picnic site and, farther down, the base area, he skirted a stand of aspen trees that grew up in a clump from a narrow crack in the rocks of a side hill. Just above, a group of Douglas fir trees stood proudly. Their massive roots plunged into and out of the rocky ground all around, grasping any chance at a bite into the soil for a chance at nourishment.

On the upturned root ball of one wind-toppled tree, Daniel caught movement out of the corner of his eye. Sure enough, a blue grouse walked along the trunk, paying him no mind. It strutted away, then turned and came back toward him. Without any idea that he was there, the bird was simply passing the time of day.

Daniel slowly ducked down behind a large tree and shucked his backpack. He quietly worked the zipper on the main pouch and produced a wrist-rocket sling shot. For years, he'd carried the primitive weapon with him on mountain hunts. It was an effective tool for killing grouse and other small game without spooking anything else in the woods. Nearly silent, a slingshot could be used in very close proximity to elk and deer without them being alerted.

He felt around on the ground between the exposed roots for a few stones. Often, when a tree root burst out of a crack in the rocky ground, it shattered the stones around it and left small tailings. These worked perfectly as slingshot ammunition. Daniel found two nickel-sized pieces and scooped them up, then headed for the grouse.

With one stone, he hit the bird right at the

base of its neck, stunning it and causing it to fall off the log. Just as it regained its footing, Daniel was on it with another stone, this time at closer range. He held it by the neck as it died in a flurry of fading wingbeats, then dressed the bird by stepping on its wings and pulling on its feet.

All that remained was a perfect ribcage and the breast meat. He put the warm carcass in a plastic bag and tucked it into his pack. Just as he was about to head back to camp, Daniel caught movement a little farther along the ridge.

He pulled up his binoculars in time to see a coyote bounding through a gap in the trees. This was not surprising. Coyotes have an outstanding sense of smell and were hearty scavengers. It was likely that this dog had simply caught wind of some blood in the air, then had come to investigate.

The coyote, a beautiful specimen with thick winter fur already beginning to grow, seemed not to believe its eyes as it rounded the aspen grove and came face-to-face with Daniel. In another situation, it would've been an easy choice for him. Coyote pelts were selling well in the far east. Today, though, Daniel decided to let the dog walk.

I don't need any more scent around my campsite, Daniel thought. *Especially with blood-thirsty mountain lions trying to hang me on their meat pole.*

Later, at camp, he dined on fried grouse breast and instant brown rice. The protein would do him some good—he had a lot of hiking to do in the coming days.

Chapter Thirteen

A week passed without anything noteworthy on the mountain lion front. Daniel covered new ground each day and spied all manner of game in the hills. He snuck up on a herd of elk one afternoon as they basked in the warm sunshine. Two camp robbers seemed to have adopted him, and they followed him through the timber every day, flitting from one branch to another like tiny fighter jets. He grew to enjoy their company.

He hadn't seen a single track or found a lion-killed carcass in seven days. The big, deadly cat that had stalked him on his first hike seemed to have disappeared from the area, but Daniel couldn't rest on that. He felt like he was being watched constantly.

Years of experience caused him to recognize the feeling and honor it rather than cast it aside as a trick of the mind. He knew something wasn't right. Each night, as he nestled into his sleeping bag, a recurring thought tugged on the corners of his confidence.

The lion was simply biding its time.

On the eighth day of his dry spell, Daniel returned to his camp just before darkness overtook the meadow. He changed into a pair of sweat pants, leaving his holstered pistol on the belt of his hunting pants, then started a fire. Tonight's menu featured a cottontail rabbit he killed earlier on his hike, which he would roast over the coals, and a hearty serving of instant mashed potatoes. With the fire burning steadily, he took up a small aluminum pot and headed for the creek.

When he bent down to fill his pot with water for boiling, he thought he caught a slight movement out of the corner of his eye. An eerie feeling came over him, like a cold dusting of snow down the back of his neck. It was almost completely dark in the meadow by then and he couldn't be sure, but he stood still for a moment to confirm that the coast was clear. For a few long minutes, he made a detailed examination of his campsite. Nothing seemed amiss.

You're getting jumpy, he scolded. *Why would anything be here, where your scent and noise have been for the last ten days? The animals that were here have left. You haven't seen any deer or rabbits in the meadow for days.*

Just as quickly as he shamed himself, he knew the answer. *You're not crazy. You're unarmed, out in the open, and a man-eating cat is prowling around somewhere. You might be stupid, but you're not crazy.*

Going an entire week without seeing one of

the big predators had allowed Daniel to grow complacent. He should've worn his pistol to the creek. Standing in the water, he recalled old magazine stories about Alaskan bear hunters whose lives had been saved by their sidearm. The hunters' advice was always the same: never go anywhere without a gun.

A few more painfully slow minutes passed as he stood, eyeing his camp. Finally, he decided that standing in the open was more dangerous than making a dash for the tent. He took up his full water pot in one hand and a large rock in the other, then strode across the meadow with false confidence.

At the tent, he quickly strapped on his holster and unsnapped the thumb break. He stoked the fire until it cast a glow around the entire meadow. Nothing seemed to be out of place. His dinner might be crispy, being cooked over high flames instead of low coals, but he didn't mind. Crunchy rabbit was a small price to pay for peace of mind. As quickly as he could, Daniel wolfed down his meal without tasting it. Usually, a good meal was all it took for him to feel like himself after a scare. Still, something gnawed at him. He was restless and his mind raced uncontrollably.

Resolved to calm his nerves once and for all, Daniel had a loud conversation with himself. He laid out all of his thoughts and doubts in full voice. His concerns came out as he thought of them. There was no order to his thinking, just a need to let it all out. Between the crackling fire and his heartfelt confession, there was little silence in the dark meadow for nearly an hour. It was a full-tilt soul-baring.

Suddenly, Daniel's eyelids got very heavy. He collapsed into the doorway of his tent and his world went dark.

He slept deeply until almost noon and woke to the sound of his camp robber pals squawking their alarm. Daniel leaned up on an elbow and rubbed the sleep from his eyes. The day was bright, and he cursed himself for falling asleep before extinguishing the fire completely with water from the creek. One errant spark could've ignited the timber surrounding his camp.

It was his own fault that the matching birds followed him around, Daniel knew. Each morning, they were given the opportunity to scour his breakfast dishes for a minute or two while he got into his hunting clothes. He'd effectively trained them to come in for a treat.

Feeding any wild creature directly was against his better judgment, but he allowed it because he enjoyed their antics and their company. In a strange way, he felt a sense of security when the two jays were around. He even named them— Toby and Tory—and spoke to them as he went around camp doing chores.

This morning, he scolded Tory for chasing

Toby away from the pot that held traces of his mashed potatoes. When the bird wouldn't relent, he walked over to pick up the dish. The birds flitted away to a nearby tree limb and squawked their disapproval. With a gentle wave, he dismissed them. Bending down to scoop up the aluminum pot, he saw a track.

In the soft earth of his campsite, between the fire and the tent, a clear print lay pressed into a damp spot in the soil. Daniel had dumped some of his creek water out of the pot before making potatoes, he remembered. The spot where the track lay was muddy because of that water. That meant that this track was made after he cooked dinner—and after he'd fallen into a deep sleep halfway inside his tent.

The track was made by a familiar animal, he noticed immediately. Normal cat tracks had four toes spaced almost evenly around a distinctly-shaped rear pad. The pad had two lobes on the front and three at the rear, like the letter "M" drawn in a bubble font. This track, however, had the middle two toes spaced far apart. He'd seen it before, up on the mountain. It was likely that the lion injured its foot as a kitten and it never healed properly. The track belonged to the cat that stalked him on the high peak. Now, it had come into his camp while he slept.

After the fight he'd witnessed, Daniel had a hunch that this cat was solely responsible for all of the construction site attacks. And now, after observing its boldness when it came into his camp, he was sure.

Daniel started shaking like a leaf. If he didn't kill this cat soon, he thought, Hanco would have one more dead worker on its hands.

He sat down on a log, unable to stand on failing knees. His body shook and his breath came in gasps. The sound of a rapid heartbeat filled Daniel's ears. It took a few minutes of concentration and shallow breathing before he managed to regain his composure.

Slowly, his mind began to work in its regular, methodical manner.

If the cat knows where I am and it knows my routine, it's not going to wait around, he thought. *I wouldn't.*

His mind went back to his ambush training in the deer woods of North Dakota.

When a buck gives you an opportunity, you don't waste it. You make the shot the first time you have a chance. This cat won't wait long.

Daniel replayed everything that had happened since he arrived at Highland Peak. Little things, like the coyote running toward him after he'd killed the grouse, were viewed through a new lens. When he spotted the bull moose, was it standing in the open by choice, or had something forced it from the dark timber? He had to look at each event through a different, more sinister lens.

Now he had to ask... *what if the cat had caused it to happen that way?*

Chapter Fourteen

For the remainder of the day, Daniel pored over his journal and his map. He drew lines to show where he'd already been across the unfolded page with a felt-tipped marker, not caring if it interfered with the map's topographic contour lines or drainage names. This was no longer about exploring new country—it was about dissecting the old ground.

He carefully studied each day's journey in his memory, trying to recall exactly what happened. In places where he stopped to glass or to hunt small game, he drew a circle on the map. When every movement of his trip had been accounted for, he built a makeshift easel out of sticks in front of his tent, then tied the map to it and leaned back on his bunched-up sleeping bag.

Daniel wanted to view the map from a distance so he could find a pattern—any pattern—in the lines. At first, there seemed to be nothing predictable in his routine. Each day he went a different direction at a different elevation. Checking his notes, he saw that the wind was in his face most of the time, which was a hunting technique he used confidently. That was the one constant on his map now.

"Always keep the wind in your face, kiddo," his father's friend Les had told him years ago, on learning that Daniel would be taking a trip to southeastern Montana for a mule deer hunt. "They can't smell you if you can smell them," the wizened older man had said casually.

Suddenly, something clicked in Daniel's mind. *I'm not the hunter! I'm the prey!*

He ripped the map from the easel and looked more closely. Sure enough, there was a pattern. It was not difficult to discern where the wind was coming from, which was how Daniel had been looking at it. More challenging to decipher, though, was where the wind was carrying his scent. Viewed this way, he could see the pattern now, clear as a mountain stream.

The cat was an expert hunter. Each day, it caught wind of his movements as the thermals fell. Then, as he came out on the mountain face somewhere, thermal currents rose with the heat of the day. When Daniel dropped into a drainage to look for what the cat might be stalking, it seemed content to follow him on an elevated ridge, catching his scent as it blew up the slope.

Looking again, Daniel could see that he'd been very vulnerable several times over the last week. From the first day, the lion had tracked him on the ridge. It was likely that when he'd stopped to kill the grouse down by the picnic spot, the cat was watching. The predator could've also followed him to the saddle where the fight raged with the bull elk. The small circles he'd drawn didn't meet, but they did come close.

Daniel bristled as he considered what might've happened if the elk hadn't been there first, or if the coyote hadn't been nearby. It didn't take much for a hunter to call off a stalk—he'd done it numerous times for one reason or another. He had to assume that the big mountain lion was no different. If one small thing went wrong, the cat simply decided to wait.

Now that he knew what the lion knew about him, he examined the map more deeply. It was a deadly chess match they were playing. If he moved one way, the cat would move in a corresponding fashion. It was the only predictable thing the lion did, and Daniel planned to exploit it.

Assuming anything about a fully-grown animal's movements was a big risk. Many times in his youth, he'd been tricked by a big buck that followed a routine. Like clockwork, he'd seen the animal come on a regular route at a regular time for days in a row. Each time, it seemed like he was only a few yards off with his stand placement or timing, but got closer to punching his tag every day.

Finally, when he was sure the kill was eminent, the deer would trick him. Sometimes it would come out in a completely different location, somewhere that never crossed his mind. There were times when he would've sworn the buck he was hunting was a ghost. One minute, it was nowhere to be seen, and the next minute, it was past him and out of range. Those big deer were champions of survival.

This cat certainly qualified as a champion hunter—it had attacked six men. The trick was for Daniel to be ready when the cat decided to make its move, and to make a good shot. If he didn't, the chances of him making it back to civilization in one piece were very slim.

He planned a deliberate set of movements for the following day. The route was designed to give him ample exposure, which was a double-edged sword. Thermal currents would carry his scent exactly where he wanted it, which was good. The downside was that there was less available cover for him to use as a defense tactic, should the lion try to take him in open country. Something as simple as a single tree could be used as an obstacle, giving him a fraction of a second to regain his composure, steady his aim, and possibly save his life.

Daniel was going to use himself as bait for the vicious lion—live bait.

The sheer lunacy of his plan made him grin. Most people never saw a mountain lion in their lifetime, and Daniel was purposely putting himself in the path of one. Clearly, the cat he was hunting had decided to turn the tables on him and would kill him if the opportunity was there. He intended to give it that chance, then beat it at its own game.

Chapter Fifteen

The realization that his next few days were dedicated to survival—and little else—struck Daniel in a strange way. He didn't feel sad or angry at all. There were no homesick thoughts of his family or Marissa, nor were there any thoughts of surrender. A strange feeling of calm came over him instead. Up to this point in his career, nothing had stopped him from doing his work.

This was a more dangerous situation than he'd encountered before. He did some mental gymnastics to come up with a plan of attack, to look at the situation in a completely different way. It was uncomfortable and a bit scary. This would be his toughest test yet, but he knew he was up for the challenge. A little self-confidence went a long way when he was alone in the wilderness.

Daniel's career was something he crafted. There was no job description in a school counselor's book, no aptitude test that recommended chasing dangerous animals in dangerous places. His qualifications were not printed on a certificate or diploma. The only true measurements of his ability were the demand for his services and the amount his clients were willing to pay. Both were high.

His mind drifted back to the stories he'd read about professional hunters in Africa. Dusty books about the exploits of those masters of the bush, often found deep in the stacks at the public library, had comprised the majority of his reports in school. He loved reading about other hunters' experiences, and had envisioned himself in each story alongside the author. As he reminisced, one story came to the forefront of his memory.

The focus of the story was a safari hunter—a professional hunter's client—Daniel recalled. The man had wounded a male lion with a poorly-placed shot, and the P.H., the guide, had gone into a thick stand of brush to finish the job. The client remembered hearing two shots, then a low roar. His shouts to the P.H. went unanswered. Moments later, with the native trackers alongside him, he discovered a grisly scene.

The lion and the P.H. lay motionless in a tangle of bodies and blood. A set of puncture marks at the guide's throat pumped blood, but he clung to life. The lion was dead, with three bullet holes and, as a last-ditch effort, a massive knife wound just behind its thick mane. The professional hunter's Bowie knife lay nearby, covered in blood.

Cats were tough, Daniel knew. The lion in Africa was much bigger than its counterpart in

North America, but bigger didn't always mean better. A full-grown mountain lion could take down game much bigger than itself—including humans. With a single misstep, his fate would be similar to that of the African P.H.

There's no going back, he thought. *You're in this thing.*

Make sure you don't miss.

Chapter Sixteen

Setting out on what he hoped would be the final morning of his hunt, Daniel made no effort to be stealthy. He cracked branches beneath his boots, brushed his pack against noisy tree bark, and even spent some time whistling. Toby and Tory flitted along with him, eagerly racing one another to the next tree limb up the trail. Their exploits amused him.

Daniel had spent so much time in the wilderness depending on his ability to be quiet that it required a conscious effort for him to do the opposite. He came to enjoy it, and tromped back and forth through a small stream like a young child in a mud puddle. A grin appeared on his face and stuck there as he followed his designed route, out in the most open patches of ground between the picnic area and the mountaintop.

Every time he stopped to listen, he heard nothing out of the ordinary. The jays said their piece from a nearby log or boulder, and the wind sang gently through the trees. The morning sun was warm on his face.

When he got to the picnic area, Daniel climbed atop the logs of the table and pulled his binoculars up. Far to the south, he could barely make out a cluster of trailers. The base area was only a few miles from him, but it seemed a world away. He hadn't seen another human being for almost two weeks. His voice, out of practice, cracked whenever he spoke to the camp-robbers. He hadn't showered or shaved or combed his hair since the night before he met Greg.

Poor guy, he thought. Greg was probably having to answer all kinds of questions about what Hanco was doing to take care of the deadly problem.

And what could he tell them? Could he say that Hanco had hired a young kid to kill off the offending cats? That, no, there was no way the cat hunter could be reached for comment? Would the press just take Hanco's word for it that the problem was being solved in a humane way?

Daniel liked Greg Ludlow, and wanted to see him succeed. It occurred to him that, if the cat problem was not solved soon, the Highland Peak project might be abandoned. Each day the resort went without vacationers paying the bills was a day closer to bankruptcy. Greg, as the public face of the outfit, would be crucified in the media if the project were scrapped. He would be viewed as incompetent, and would surely be fired.

I can't let that happen, Daniel thought. *I've got to*

bring this cat in, and the sooner I do it, the better it is for Greg. And for me.

The air around Daniel's perch on the picnic table seemed to die in an instant. Where a light breeze had been, suddenly nothing stirred. The sun beat down on his face from above, and small beads of perspiration formed along his brow. Even the faithful jays, Toby and Tory, were nowhere to be found. An eerie, nervous feeling overtook him, and Daniel noticed that his palms were sweating.

Some called it "the calm before the storm." Others referred to it as "butterflies in your stomach." Like an athlete before a big game, or a motorcycle racer on the starting gate, Daniel's senses went into overdrive. He crouched slowly and reached for his pistol, then considered the situation.

Cautiously, Daniel worked his pistol around to the front of his body. He still faced south, where the wind had been headed. His scent and noise had preceded him to the picnic area, and the cat had surely found him. The question now, though, was not an easy one. Where was the lion?

Thinking back, Daniel remembered how the cat had climbed a tree and waited for him up on the summit. Also, the lion had ambushed the bull elk from above. It made perfect sense that somewhere nearby—probably within striking distance—the man-eating cat was watching and waiting for him to make the next move.

Then he heard the noise.

Chapter Seventeen

It was a faint sound, but not so faint that it went unnoticed. There was no snapping twig or rustling leaves, just a soft rolling noise that carried on the still air in the clearing. It reminded Daniel of the sound of an underinflated bicycle tire rolling down a paved road. The noise only occurred for a second, but it was distinct. Daniel's suspicions had been confirmed—the lion was nearby, watching him.

He cautiously slid his feet down to the matted grass below the picnic table's log bench and gained his footing. Both hands still grasped the gun, and he adjusted his grip. Any moment he could be called on to use the weapon. He wanted to be ready—his life depended on it.

After standing still for five minutes, he commenced walking north, toward the high-reaching mountaintop. He scanned the clearing's edge as he strode along. Here and there, a rock ledge jutted up from the densely forested slope.

It's in the rocks, Daniel thought. *That sound had to be the cat's pads on stone, not bark or grass.*

His stiff muscles quickly limbered as he neared the edge of the clearing. One of the rocky outcroppings rose in front of him. His discerning eye picked the patch of stone apart as he moved.

Well, the cat's not in that one, Daniel decided. He would've seen it.

Five steps later, his heart nearly leapt out of his chest. There, standing above him on the jagged rock, was a very big, angry tomcat. It screamed at him with all the fury in the world, and a chill ran down Daniel's spine. He tried to remain calm, but knew that with one leap the animal could close the scant 20-foot distance between them. The lion had decided that this was where they would meet.

Daniel readjusted his right hand and eased the hammer back, never taking his eyes off the cat. This was the moment he'd imagined every night since Hanco contacted him. He was face to face with a mountain lion.

Finally, when the cat could take no more, it pounced toward him with another awful, beautiful scream. Daniel raised his gun, aiming instinctively. He didn't see his sights at all. When he fired, he never heard the shot.

The massive animal had sprung on its last victim. Daniel's .44 hit it squarely in the chest, then exited through its back, severing its spine on the way out. The cat landed with a heavy thud three feet from Daniel's boots. Acting on autopilot, he quickly regained his senses and delivered a coup-de-grace to the back of the animal's head. The taxidermist would have to do some serious stitching to make the cat presentable, but Daniel wasn't going to take any chances. He needed to be certain that this lion was dead.

He backed away slowly and sat on the grass. Ten yards from him lay the animal responsible for many deaths and millions of lost dollars, unable to wreak any more havoc. The resolution to Hanco's problem had been a shy prairie kid with a healthy body, a healthy mind, and the nerve to use both.

He watched the fallen cat for a long time. Sometimes, he came upon animals in the throes of death and had a hard time with it. One cow elk in Colorado had clung to life like a spider to its web, its sides heaving for minutes after a final bullet had ended the brain's ability to register pain. Daniel had cried over that cow. He didn't take death lightly.

This lion, however, showed no signs of life. The breeze in the meadow had regained its strength, and tousled the bristled tail fur of the deadly predator. Toby and Tory reappeared and made their presence known from atop a nearby boulder. Daniel guessed that they were anxious for a chance at the carcass before any other scavengers could arrive.

Chapter Eighteen

Daniel went to bed without supper that night. Part of him had wanted to take a section of loin from the cat and roast it over the fire. Mountain lion could be eaten and was very tasty if properly prepared. Trichinosis, a roundworm parasite, was known to exist in mountain lions, but was harmless to humans if the meat reached a high enough temperature. Daniel had eaten mountain lion before and had suffered no ill effects.

The fact that this particular cat had been dining on human flesh, though, gave him pause. It made it easier for him to leave the skinned carcass in the meadow, where all manner of wild creatures could use the meat without any moral objection. His job was nearly finished, and it had been an emotional journey. Desire to see the job completed would be enough sustenance for the rest of his time on the mountain.

He awoke early the next morning and packed up his humble camp. All the freeze-dried food was now gone, and the wrappers fit neatly into the bottom of his bag. His tent, bedroll, and cooking gear fit snugly inside as well. With the hunt over, Daniel strapped his rifle to the outside of his pack. He wouldn't be able to reach it there, but it made no difference—any long-range work was done, and he still wore his pistol for protection.

Mounting his pack, Daniel took a last look around the little basin he'd called home. Sunlight shone down through the treetops above the creek, reflecting brightly on the water. High above the trees, the tall peak stood silhouetted in the morning light. It was a beautiful day in the mountains. As he started back on the trail to the base area, Toby and Tory joined up and led the way.

He proceeded down the mountain with the cat's hide slung over his pack like a trophy. When he walked through the construction site at the bottom of the mountain, he envisioned all the men who would soon be back to work. He thought of all the families who would vacation in the area now that it was safe.

Daniel spent half a month hunting—and being hunted. He'd saved Hanco millions of dollars in delays and settlement monies, while making plenty for himself. He made the mountain safe for its workers, and enjoyed himself in the process. Even the hard times, the moments when his nerves had been on the ragged edge, were enjoyable after the fact. Like a good hockey goalie that lets in a bad shot, a good hunter needed to have a short memory sometimes. A man had to simply forget the bad things—like he'd done with Marissa—in order to be effective.

At the base, Daniel took a much-needed shower in the foreman's office trailer, then picked up the telephone and punched in Greg's number. The two arranged to meet at the nearby office of the Wyoming Game and Fish Department to seal the cat's hide. After everything was legal, they would go into town and grab a bite to eat.

When he wheeled his trusty pickup truck into the parking lot, Greg was already there. He sported a two-week growth of whiskers on his face, and his skin was the ruddy red of a weathered outdoorsman. The shiny SUV he stood next to now sported a mud-covered paintjob that was similar to the one on Daniel's rig. Greg's fancy boots were now well worn.

As he got out of the truck, Greg came over and extended a hand.

"My goodness, Daniel, I'm glad you're safe and sound," the company man said, clapping Daniel on the shoulder as they shook. "How the heck are you?"

"I'm fine, Greg. You look like mountain life suits you," Daniel responded, pointing at Greg's boots. "Did you decide to take up a new career as a boot destroyer?" he joked.

"I love it here. As a matter of fact, I've decided that I'm going to stay," Greg replied. "I've been hiking a lot between media interviews," he said quietly, a broad grin creasing his face.

The pair went into the department office and summoned a conservation officer to check out the lion hide. They dutifully signed an affidavit to the legitimacy of the kill. At Daniel's request,

Greg had informed the local law enforcement of Daniel's hunt at Highland Peak, and there were no hiccups.

The hunter, the company man, and the conservation officer stood around Daniel's tailgate for a long while, visiting about fishing, hunting, and the Highland Peak project. When their figures cast a long shadow on the gravel parking lot, the men finally parted with a handshake.

Chapter Nineteen

Daniel dropped the hide off at a local taxidermist's shop, one that the man from Game and Fish had used and recommended highly. Hanco would have their stuffed mountain lion in about three months. After that, he followed Greg's directions to a small bistro on the edge of Jackson Hole. Inside, Greg had taken a table at the rear and was waiting for him.

The two men ordered meals on Hanco's dime, then proceeded to catch up about the events of the last few weeks. While Daniel had been nearly silent, Greg's time had been full of conversation with the media. His job as the mouthpiece for Hanco Ventures required quotes early and often.

"I had the news outfits on me every day, poking me like a bear in a cage," Greg started. "But, after you went back in the hills, I didn't have anything new to tell them about the situation."

"I imagine it gets frustrating," Daniel said. "Having all those vultures around, looking to take your words and twist them must be stressful."

"It really was, at first," Greg said. "But then, a funny thing happened—I went fishing for the first time since I was a kid."

"You went fishing?" Daniel asked.

"Yep, I went fishing. I couldn't stand the garbage they were printing about me—and about you—anymore. I was ready to quit this job, to move back to Houston. Problem was, you were still out there," Greg said.

When Daniel didn't respond, Greg continued.

"I couldn't just leave you to deal with the press, so I decided to stick it out.

"I walked into one of these fancy fly shops and hired a guide to take me one afternoon. We went way back through the hills and fished a stretch of river that he'd never floated before. It was a beautiful day. We really hammered the fish, too. As many as I've ever caught. It was fantastic!"

Daniel smiled, responding, "That's great, Greg, but what does that have to do with making your job easier?"

"Well, I'll tell you. I went out away from the circus, and I saw the mountains. I mean, I really saw them. We saw deer and elk, eagles, even a few otters on the river. It was like a whole new world opened up. So, the next time a journalist asked me for an interview, I took them fishing, too.

"Next thing you know, I'm yapping on and on about the virtues of clean, sustainable living in the west," Greg said, smiling. Seeing Daniel's quizzical look, he explained. "Sometimes I get a little carried away."

Daniel could see that his friend was trying to downplay it, but it was clear that the mountains had taken hold of him. His face beamed as he showed Daniel some pictures of the trout he'd caught in the past few weeks.

"So, Greg, you're now an advocate for clean mountain living, huh?" Daniel asked.

"I guess so," Greg replied. "One of the reporters caught me on tape talking about the wilderness, and they put it on the internet. Next thing you know, Hanco's board has promoted me to Vice President of Operations for Highland

Peak. I'm done with Houston—I'm their guy in
Wyoming now." His smile was a mile wide.

"Congratulations, Greg," Daniel said. "I'm
glad you're staying here—they'll need a bona fide
mountain man at the helm."

Their food arrived, and the two men sat
quietly for a moment, taking the opportunity to
give thanks. Then they flew into their plates like
only those with an outdoors-induced appetite
could. They ordered seconds, then dessert. Finally
full, they pushed away from the table and
meandered up and down the main drag of
Jackson Hole for a while.

Hanco had arranged for Daniel to stay at a
fancy hotel that evening, and he gladly accepted.
The lodging was on the far end of town, just a
block off the main thoroughfare. Daniel wheeled
his truck into the parking area, followed closely
by Greg's SUV. After checking in with the owner,
the men pulled up chairs in a nicely-appointed

drawing room to handle business. Greg wrote Daniel a check for $20,000. When Daniel protested, Greg chuckled.

"I know that's more than you think you're owed, but it's far less than what I think you should be paid," he said. "You've saved this company several million dollars. The way you did it was exactly how it should be done, with no wasted wildlife." Greg lowered his voice and smiled as he said, "If anyone asks, tell them your incidental expenses were very high."

Never one to look a gift horse in the mouth, Daniel graciously accepted the payment and bid goodbye to his friend. They made plans to do some fishing the following summer.

The next morning, Daniel loaded up his truck and made his way out of town. His next job was waiting for him. As he drove down the canyon, the unseasonably warm Indian Summer air rushed into his truck cab. He caught sight of

the ski mountain in his rearview mirror. A sense
of satisfaction came over him, and he smiled.

Five miles later, though, the road made a
sharp curve back toward Highland Peak. From
this point in the road, Daniel figured the distance
to his campsite at less than three miles. He was
closer still to where the cat had tried to kill him.
With the windows of his pickup open, he was
sure he heard the scream of a mountain lion, and
a chill ran down his spine.

ACKNOWLEDGMENTS

God, first and foremost and always.
My beautiful, supportive wife Mindy for her
patience and sharp red pen.
My family, who has always encouraged my
creative pursuits.
And to Jerry, in Big Sky.

More from Sam Finden:

Saddle My Good Horse

Lone Wolf

For more information, visit

www.SamFinden.com.

www.ingramcontent.com/pod-product-compliance
Lightning Source LLC
Chambersburg PA
CBHW020915180626
46816CB00007BA/2417